RACHAEL RAY:

FROM CANDY COUNTER TO COOKING SHOW

EXTRAORDINARY SUCCESS WITH A HIGH SCHOOL DIPLOMA OR LESS

JENNIFER ANISTON: FROM FRIENDS TO FILMS

TYRA BANKS: FROM THE RUNWAY TO THE TELEVISION SCREEN

HALLE BERRY: FROM BEAUTY QUEEN TO OSCAR WINNER

JAMES CAMERON: FROM TRUCK DRIVER TO DIRECTOR

SIMON COWELL: FROM THE MAILROOM TO IDOL FAME

ELLEN DEGENERES: FROM COMEDY CLUB TO TALK SHOW

MICHAEL DELL: FROM CHILD ENTREPRENEUR TO COMPUTER MAGNATE

STEVE JOBS: FROM APPLES TO APPS

RACHAEL RAY: FROM CANDY COUNTER TO COOKING SHOW

RUSSELL SIMMONS: FROM THE STREETS TO THE MUSIC BUSINESS

JIM SKINNER: FROM BURGERS TO THE BOARDROOM

HARRY TRUMAN: FROM FARMER TO PRESIDENT

MARK ZUCKERBERG: FROM FACEBOOK TO FAMOUS

RACHAEL RAY:

FROM CANDY COUNTER TO COOKING SHOW

by Shaina C. Indovino

Mason Crest

RACHAEL RAY: *FROM CANDY COUNTER TO COOKING SHOW*

Mason Crest
370 Reed Road
Broomall, Pennsylvania 19008
www.masoncrest.com

Printed and bound in the United States of America.

First printing
9 8 7 6 5 4 3 2 1

Library of Congress Cataloging-in-Publication Data

Indovino, Shaina Carmel.
  Rachael Ray : from candy counter to cooking show / Shaina C. Indovino.
    p. cm. — (Extraordinary success with a high school diploma or less)
  Includes index.
   ISBN 978-1-4222-2300-0 (hard cover) — ISBN 978-1-4222-2293-5 (series hardcover) — ISBN 978-1-4222-9361-4 (ebook)
 1. Ray, Rachael—Juvenile literature. 2. Cooks—United States—Biography—Juvenile literature. I. Title.
 TX649.R29I53 2012
 641.5092—dc23
 [B]
                                          2011024226

Produced by Harding House Publishing Services, Inc.
www.hardinghousepages.com
Interior design by Camden Flath.
Cover design by Torque + Design.

CONTENTS

INTRODUCTION

Finding a great job without a college degree is hard to do—but it's possible. In fact, more and more, going to college doesn't necessarily guarantee you a job. In the past few years, only one in four college graduates find jobs in their field. And, according to the U.S. Bureau of Labor Statistics, eight out of the ten fastest-growing jobs don't require college degrees.

But that doesn't mean these jobs are easy to get. You'll need to be willing to work hard. And you'll also need something else. The people who build a successful career without college are all passionate about their work. They're excited about it. They're committed to getting better and better at what they do. They don't just want to make money. They want to make money doing something they truly love.

So a good place for you to start is to make a list of the things you find really interesting. What excites you? What do you love doing? Is there any way you could turn that into a job?

Now talk to people who already have jobs in that field. How did they get where they are today? Did they go to college—or did they find success through some other route? Do they know anyone else you can talk to? Talk to as many people as you can to get as many perspectives as possible.

According to the U.S. Department of Labor, two out of every three jobs require on-the-job training rather than a college degree. So your next step might be to find an entry-level position in the field that interests you. Don't expect to start at the top. Be willing to learn while you work your way up from the bottom.

That's what almost all the individuals in this series of books did: they started out somewhere that probably seemed pretty distant from their end goal—but it was actually the first step in their journey. Celebrity Simon Cowell began his career working in a mailroom. Jim Skinner, who ended up running McDonald's Corporation, started out flipping burgers. World-famous cook Rachael Ray worked at a candy counter. All these people found incredible success without a college degree—but they all had a dream of where they wanted to go in life . . . and they were willing to work hard to make their dream real.

Ask yourself: Do I have a dream? Am I willing to work hard to make it come true? The answers to those questions are important!

CHAPTER 1
EARLY INFLUENCE

Words to Know

formal: Formal means going along with the usual rules and requirements for doing something.
collaborate: To collaborate is to work together on.
innovative: If something is innovative it is something new that's never been done before.
culinary: Culinary means having to do with cooking.

In 2006, Rachael Ray was given an opportunity that most of us only dream about. Without any *formal* training whatsoever, Rachael Ray was offered her own talk show—and not by just anyone! Oprah Winfrey had heard about Rachael's amazing success as a television host on *30 Minute Meals*, and Oprah loved her personality. She wanted to extend the invitation to *collaborate* on a cooking show they both would produce, but Rachael Ray would host. As anyone can guess—Rachael agreed!

In less than ten years, Rachael went from being a rather unknown manager at an upscale grocery store to becoming a talk-show host that pulled in over a million viewers each day. Not only that; she also gets to meet incredibly famous and successful people each time she hosts a show. The list of guests she has had on her show is seemingly endless, including hundreds of easily recognizable names. But what *really* makes her life extraordinary isn't the fact that she has her own talk show; plenty of people do. It's the fact that she never formally learned how to be a professional chef—she never went to college at all, in fact—and yet she is making more money and gaining more publicity than most people that cook for a living.

Her lively, bubbly personality makes her fun to watch and learn from. Her **innovative** techniques for cooking quick and easy meals makes her viewers want to cook right alongside her. To many people, cooking is hard, but Rachael does everything with you, right down to chopping the ingredients.

Rachael's tale is not ordinary by any means. To truly appreciate where she is now, you need to know where she came from.

Early Life

Rachael Ray was born on August 25, 1968, in Glens Falls, New York. Both her parents came from very culturally rich backgrounds. Her mother is an Italian-American, and her father is a mixture of French, Scottish, and Welsh. Their different backgrounds exposed them to all sorts of dishes, and boy, did they love to cook! Some of Rachael's first memories are of watching her family preparing meals in the kitchen. Even though she is a successful television star today, she still thinks her family is much better than she is when it comes to cooking.

Shortly after Rachael was born, her family moved several hours away to Cape Cod, Massachusetts. Her parents owned and operated several different restaurants there. Rachael spent

Rachael was born in Glens Falls, a town of around 15,000 people in New York State.

Rachael grew up spending a lot of time at her parents' Cape Cod, Massa-chusetts restaurants.

a lot of time in those restaurants when she was young. According to family legend, Rachael's first word was *vino* the Italian word for "wine." (Wine is a popular cooking ingredient in Italian cuisine.) Rachael was never taught how to do anything formally; she just learned by observing. In fact, she spent so much time around people cooking that she absorbed most of it without having to ask any questions.

Of course, she wasn't born an experienced cook! One time, when she was only about three of four, she saw her mother using a spatula, so she tried to mimic her mother—but ended up burning herself while trying to flip hot cheese. Not surprisingly, this painful incident is one of her earliest memories.

Even from an early age, Rachael had her hand in preparing meals. It became a way of life for her. She also had several other passions, though. Her parents say she was always very focused and hardworking when it came to something she loved. She enjoyed drawing and sometimes retreated to be alone to do that. She was always enthusiastic about anything that interested her. Years later, this part of her personality really spilled over into her television presence!

Rachael had two siblings, and they all learned to cook early in life. Their mother would often bring her children with her to the restaurant where she worked. Sometimes, she'd even have them help prepare the food. Today, all the Ray kids have their specialties. Maria is the best at baking—something Rachael has admitted she is terrible at! Manny is great at slow-cooking. Rachael's strength comes from her ability to take complex meals and simplify them so that anyone can prepare them.

Rachael's family moved again when she was eight years old. This time, they moved to Lake George, New York, where she would spend the rest of her childhood. Her mother began working in the restaurant business again in the upstate New York town, which meant that Rachael still had a lot of hands-on experience in the professional cooking world.

Everyone in Rachael's family cooks, with no exceptions! Some take more pride in it than others, but they all grew up surrounded by it. One thing that makes Rachael's family extremely special is the fact that her ancestors come from very diverse areas of the world. Her maternal grandfather, whose ancestors were from Sicily, often cooked for his family of twelve while they were growing up. He even grew most of his own ingredients, too. Meanwhile, Rachael's father's side of the family specializes in Louisiana-style cooking, which makes his meals have more of a Southern taste. The influence from both sides of her family helped to develop Rachael's broad spectrum of knowledge in the **culinary** world before she even thought about turning it into a career.

The College Choice

Rachael's upbringing didn't really push her to go to college. Her parents were successful enough in the restaurant business that she didn't feel too much need to go to college and get a diploma. Despite that, she enrolled at Pace University in New York City. However, she didn't finish her degree. She dropped out and never returned. Instead, she spent some time at her home in Lake George.

After leaving college, Rachael spent time in Lake George, New York.

In a sense, she sort of skipped the point in her life where going to college was important. The majority of college students are fresh out of high school. Rachael's original plan was to wait until she earned enough money to go back to college, but that all changed a few years later, when she found her true calling. College seems suddenly unimportant when you're already making a lots of money doing what you love!

During her brief time in college, her majors were literature and communications. She wasn't sure what she wanted to do with her life at that point. She never considered that cooking might be her career. She had absolutely no formal training as a professional chef.

Pace University has a number of buildings throughout New York City and the surrounding areas.

Of course, college works out really well for many people; they earn a degree in the field they wish to pursue and they move on to great things.

For Rachael, however, not having any formal education is one of things that helped make her the great host she is today. Her viewers like the fact that she's just an ordinary person. Very few people watching her show are going to have a culinary degree, so why should she? After all, you don't need a degree to know how to make quick, easy, tasteful meals!

CHAPTER 2
FINDING HER PASSION

Words to Know

gourmet: Gourmet means having to do with food that's suitable for people who only like the finest foods.

It wasn't until almost ten years after graduating from high school that Rachael Ray felt the urge to try out urban life again. The small town upstate where she lived didn't offer a lot of opportunities, so she thought she'd try her luck in New York City. She set out on this new adventure in 1995 when she was in her late twenties.

Rachael's first job after arriving in New York was at a Macy's department store. She saw the job description in the classified ads and was hired to work at a candy counter. Little did her employers know that she would soon be a culinary sensation!

Rachael really showed promise, though, and she moved up the ranks quickly. From her Macy's job she learned a lot of the information she hadn't acquired at home. For instance, she learned about the business end of cooking and got some hands-on experience with dealing with people in a store setting.

Because she was so good with people, it wasn't long before she was promoted to being the manager of the fresh-foods department. Then, after two years of working at Macy's, Rachael was offered yet another promotion, but she turned it down. The Macy's management wanted to move her to an area outside of food, which she was beginning to really enjoy. So, instead of taking the promotion, she applied to a job at another store known as Agata & Valentina. This had a more **gourmet** feel than Macy's, and for a time, she was extremely happy there.

Unfortunately, Rachael's personal life wasn't going as well as her career. A few bad things happened during this phase of her life. While having a bad breakup with her boyfriend, she happened to break her ankle. Then, she was mugged outside of her apartment building in Queens, not once, but twice. Talk about a string of bad luck! Rachael didn't want to stick around to find out what would happen next.

Tired of the city life, Rachael made the choice to move back to Lake George and explore other career options there. All the bad events happening to her felt like a sign that she should not be in New York City anymore—and boy was she right! Although it certainly wasn't a good period in her life, it did send her in the right direction. After all, she might not be as successful as she is now without that extra push that got her out of New York City, sending her back home where new opportunities were waiting for her.

Rachael worked at Agata & Valentina while living in New York City.

Rising Up

After arriving back in Lake George, Rachael took a series of management positions at local pubs and bars. Lake George is a well-known vacation spot, so business there can be pretty busy all year-round. Eventually, she was hired as a buyer for Cowan & Lobel, a local food store in nearby Albany. Then she also became a stand-in cook, preparing the precooked meals sold at the store. It turned out that she was great at this.

This was a huge change from what she had been doing before; now, not only did she get to play a major role in which

For many people, buying dinner from the frozen food section of the super-market makes life easier. Rachael knew that cooking good food didn't have to take a lot of time or hard work!

items were stocked on the shelves, but she got to prepare food, too—and that was no small order! Preparing precooked food for stores often means preparing hundreds of pounds of fresh, quality food each day. Rachael rose to the occasion with enthusiasm.

Then she decided to take her job title to the next level. She noticed that more and more people were buying precooked meals instead of groceries from Cowan & Lobel. Although it was flattering to her cooking, it wasn't very good for business. Grocery stores make less money on precooked meals than they do on raw ingredients, mostly because of the labor and extra ingredients involved in making meals.

Rachael had been cooking her whole life, and she didn't understand why other people wouldn't want to cook their own meals. She went on a mission to figure out exactly why. If she could figure out how to get people to cook for themselves, she would be able to boost grocery sales and spread the joy of cooking.

She started asking various customers directly: "Why are you mostly buying precooked meals?"

Almost everyone's response was the same: "I don't have enough time to cook. Buying the precooked meals is just easier!"

Rachael knew that if you cooked a meal right, it didn't have to take longer than thirty minutes to prepare. The only problem was that not everyone knew how to cook a meal as fast as she did. So she came up with the idea of having a class to teach people how to cook meals just as fast as she could.

Becoming a Great Teacher—By Accident!

As part of a holiday promotion, Rachael sold coupons for cooking classes on how to make six thirty-minute meals. It seemed like a great idea at the time, but there was just one problem: she couldn't find a chef to teach the class at an affordable price. After much searching for an instructor, her boss suggested that she should be the one to teach the class.

Although cooking felt natural to her, teaching an entire class of people did not! The idea made her very nervous at first. After all, she wasn't a "real" chef; she was just an ordinary person. Despite her nervousness, she decided to give it a chance.

Why Thirty-Minute Meals?

It takes a delivery man about thirty minutes or more to cook your food and deliver it to your house from the moment you decide you want it. It is for this reason that plenty of people decide to order in rather than make their own meals. It's simply more convenient! No one wants to slave over a hot stove for hours just to make one meal, especially if they've worked a long day. Rachael knew this—and she figured thirty-minute meals would inspire a lot of people to start cooking again. If people are willing to wait thirty minutes for a pizza, they could easily wait thirty minutes for their own meal to be done.

Because pasta and chicken were popular sales items, Rachael decided to plan her class around a Mediterranean theme that would call for pasta and chicken ingredients. She would teach her students how to cook five different variations of six dishes, making a total of thirty unique dishes.

Rachael started her thirty-minute meal classes based around the idea that it takes about half an hour for most food deliveries.

Her first thirty-minute class was a major hit. People loved it—and they wanted more! She began to gain popularity. A local newspaper picked up Rachael's story and published it in an article. Not long after the newspaper article, she was offered a weekly thirty-minute segment on a local news station. She started touring local grocery stores, teaching others about the magic of quick, delicious meals. Local fans couldn't get enough of her. It was hard to believe how good Rachael was at teaching people about cooking, considering she had never had any formal sort of training, as either a chef or a teacher!

Rachael's first book was a massive success and helped her become the star we know today!

After a while, her fans started requesting that she make a cookbook from all her recipes. She was doing so well that she began considering the idea, too—so she contacted an independent Manhattan publisher and made it happen. The first draft of her cookbook consisted of mostly photocopied recipes inspired by her family history. The final book sold over 10,000 copies in only a few weeks—and that was just in New York! Today, more than a decade later, plenty of different cookbooks have been published that are full of just Rachael's recipes, and they have sold a lot more copies than just the 10,000 she started with.

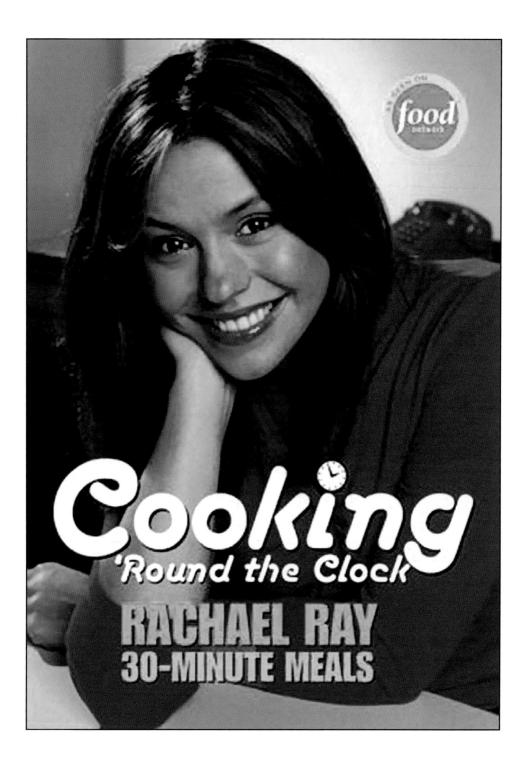

food network

Cooking
'Round the Clock

RACHAEL RAY
30-MINUTE MEALS

CHAPTER 3
BEING DISCOVERED

Words to Know
producers: Producers are the people who are responsible for overseeing how movies or television shows are made.
premiered: Premiered means showed for the first time.
debuted: Debuted means performed for the first time.
icon: An icon is a person who has become so well known that she represents a certain aspect of society.

Rachael was becoming quite a celebrity in upstate New York, but it wasn't until television **producers** started contacting her that her life really changed. Her first national appearance was on NBC's *Today* show as a guest in 2001, only a few short years after she began teaching classes.

Rachael's trip to New York City that day wasn't an easy one. A serious blizzard had rolled in across the state. This made what would normally be a four-hour drive turn into a nine-hour one. But Rachael got there. A little snow wasn't going to stop her!

A few days before this, when she had a guest appearance on a radio show, someone who knew the Food Network's senior vice

Rachael's first appearance on the Today *show with Matt Lauer helped get the attention of the Food Network and open the way for even more success for Rachael.*

president of programming overheard Rachael. That person then got in touch with someone else, and then that person discovered that Rachael would be appearing on the *Today* show. He tuned in—and was sold.

As a result, Rachael ended up with her own show. She was the host of *30-Minute Meals*, a new show to be **premiered** on the Food Network. The show **debuted** that same year, and it was a hit. By this point, Rachael already had quite a following, and now her viewer count expanded to include the entire nation.

Before Rachael Ray, most cooks featured on television were very serious about their jobs. They would dress as chefs and act the part. Rachael, on the other hand, wears normal clothes on her show, and unlike other cooking hosts, she tries to do everything her watchers will do as she prepares her meals. This means she'll cut vegetables in front of the crowd rather than have a bowl of them pre-cut and ready to use in her recipe. This method encourages the audience to follow along. It's easy to feel removed from cooking when the person instructing you on TV doesn't have nearly as hard a job as you do!

The reason so many people loved Rachael wasn't just because of her innovative thirty-minute ideas. It was also because of her personality. Rachael knows she's not an educated chef, and that makes her easy to relate to. She likes to have fun and joke around with people as she's doing what she loves—cooking. She often makes a mistake on air and then laughs it off. In fact, her very first day filming, she sliced her finger open!

Most of all, Rachael is "real." Her personality off-camera and on-camera is very much the same. She doesn't put on an act that's

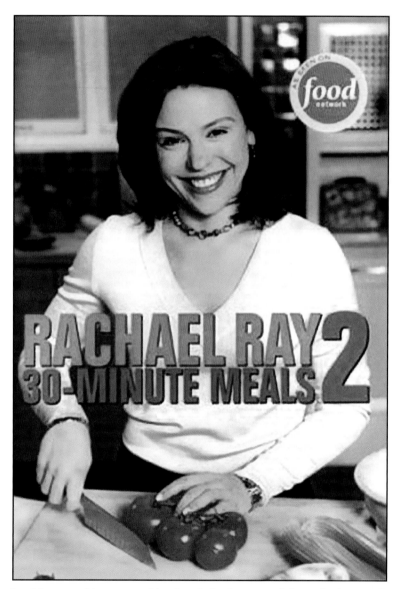

Rachael kept working on cookbooks while she gained fame for her work in television.

contrived for the show. Watching her make meals truly makes you feel like you could easily make the same meals—because you're not a professional chef either. You're an ordinary person—just like Rachael!

Why Then?

The Food Network was not a new thing. In fact, it had been around for decades hosting dozens of shows with plenty of talented (and often famous) chefs. Today, shows like *Iron Chef* have only heightened the popularity of the Food Network. But back in 2001, the executives of the company knew they needed to find a new edge. The traditional roles of husband and wife were quickly changing, and not many people had time to spend hours on one meal anymore. Both men and women were working full-time jobs, which left very little room for dedicated cooking. Not only that; not many people knew how to cook to accommodate this lifestyle. So, they simply wouldn't cook! That is where Rachael came in; she easily accommodated the needs of the twenty-first-century home.

When she first showed up for her interview at the Food Network, Rachael was very straightforward. She explained that she was not a famous or trained chef, but that was exactly why the Food Network wanted her! She would perfectly bridge the gap between high-quality cooking and the working majority of America. She was seen as the "Anti-Martha Stewart." Rachael and Martha were exact opposites, and America was ready for someone new.

Expanding a Franchise

As Rachael became more popular, her opportunities on screen increased. Not even a year after becoming the host of *30-Minute*

Meals, she was given another show: *$40 A Day*. Unlike *30-Minute Meals*, this show doesn't have Rachael cooking. In fact, it's quite the opposite! In each episode, Rachael travels to a different location and tries to survive on only $40 each day for meals. Most of the restaurants she goes to are suggested by locals, making the episode even more fun to watch. The show is a fun guide to travel, hosted by someone who is already a familiar personality. Viewers also get to learn in the process about the diversity of food across the world.

After the success of 30-Minute Meals, *Rachael had another hit with* $40 A Day.

Over the years, Rachael was given several other shows on the Food Network. These included *Inside Dish*, *Tasty Travels*, and *Rachael's Vacations*. None of these were as well known or long-standing as *30-Minute Meals*, though. Teaching people how to cook in a fun, easy way was her specialty from the start.

In 2006, Rachael won a Daytime Emmy Award for "Outstanding Service Show" and a nomination for "Outstanding Service Show Host." These were just a few of the awards she would win during her career.

In the first few years following her initial success as the host of *30-Minute Meals*, Rachael released plenty of cookbooks, making her first one part of a series. Today, there are dozens of Rachael's books on the shelves of most bookstores. Each cookbook she writes is unique. Some cater toward a certain group of people, such as vegetarians. Others have a unique recipe for each day of the year, so that every day is new and exciting. There are even several cookbooks with recipes especially for kids, making cooking fun for the whole family.

Her Many Guests

Over the course of its existence, Rachael has hosted hundreds of guests on her show. Many of her past guests are fairly well-known. Some that you might recognize are Tim Allen, Steve Carell, Miley Cyrus, Morgan Freeman, President Barack Obama, Daniel Radcliffe, Taylor Swift, and, of course, the woman who helped her start it all—Oprah Winfrey.

SNACKS TO GO page 78   STRESS-FREE DINNERS—ALL WEEK! page

EVERYDAY
WITH RACHAEL RAY

rachaelraymag.com

easy grilling

57 *fast recipes*

ALL WITH PHOTOS!

new! **30-MINUTE MEALS**

special **party guide**

TASTY BITES • COOL COCKTAILS • INSTANT DECORATING

AUGUST / SEPTEMBER 2006

Rachael has expanded her reach from books to television, and now she's moved into magazines with Everyday with Rachael Ray.

Although these were all very successful, Rachael soon came up with another idea. Why not release a subscription magazine? She did just that in 2005. She named it *Every Day with Rachael Ray*. The magazine features not only recipes by Rachael Ray but also advice on other topics surrounding dining, including where to go or what to do while enjoying your meal. Although there were not many issues released at first, the magazine's popularity steadily increased over the next few years. Today, the magazine is still going strong, and Rachael has a website to go along with it. Fans are invited to read articles and add their own two cents to the discussion.

Climbing Even Higher

In 2006, not even ten years after moving back to Lake George where she would launch her career as a local TV star, Rachael was offered a collaborative show with Oprah Winfrey. Oprah had seen Rachael on and off television, and she absolutely loved Rachael's personality; she had asked Rachael to be a guest on Oprah's own talk show several times. Together, she and Rachael would produce the show—but Rachael would be the one to host it. Rachael was at first reluctant to name the show after herself, but she eventually agreed to it. Her humble attitude has led to her being hailed as "the most down-to-earth TV star on the planet."

This was a huge step up for Rachael, sending her fame even higher than her *30-Minute Meals* slot and Daytime Emmy Award had. Now she was branching out of the cooking world into the talk-show world. Although a lot of cooking was done on the show, that wasn't all that people saw. Rachael often has

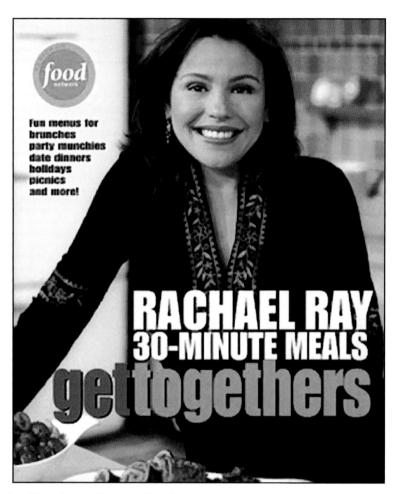

Rachael has been able to make planning and cooking delicious meals something anyone can do. Her focus on showing readers how easy cooking great food can be has inspired many new chefs to get into the kitchen.

extremely famous guests visit the set and interview with her. The show starts and ends on cooking, but the middle is filled with plenty of other activities. This talk-show style gave Rachael a much wider audience than just people who cared about cooking. Rachael Ray was starting to become an *icon* in many more communities because of this.

Millions of people watch Rachael Ray's show each day. As of 2011, the show was renewed until 2012. If it continues to be as popular as it is, there could be even more renews in the future. Rachael is an ambitious person, and she shows no signs of wanting to slow down. So far, the *Rachael Ray* show has received several Daytime Emmy Awards and has been nominated for several more.

RACHAEL RAY

2,4,6,8

GREAT MEALS FOR COUPLES OR CROWDS

AS SEEN ON food network

A 30-MINUTE MEAL COOKBOOK

CHAPTER 4
HONING HER TALENT

Words to Know

nontraditional: If something is nontraditional, it does not conform to the accepted ways of doing things.

nonprofit: Nonprofit companies are in business to help others rather than to make money.

Not long after Rachael began to host her own show, she also began to create her own unique vocabulary. She doesn't hesitate to add her own flare to cooking terminology, and her fans are not at all shy about using them. These new words are now lovingly referred to as Rachael-isms.

One of her most famously used terms is "EVOO" which stands for extra-virgin olive oil. This type of oil is extremely common in cooking, especially in Mediterranean-themed dishes. What sets this phrase apart from all her other ones is the fact that it was actually added to the *Oxford English Dictionary* in 2007! Because the word is attributed to her as the creator, she received a certificate for it. Not many people can say they've created a new word for the English language!

Other words in Rachael's personal vocabulary are combinations of two words mixed into one. "Stoup" is a combination of "soup" and "stew," a good word for a dish that is a very thick, stew-like soup. A similar word is "choup," which comes from "soup" and "chowder." "Entréetizer" is a mixture of "entrée" and "appetizer"; an entrée-tizer is a meal-sized appetizer. Rachael also has a few words that act as shortcuts on her show. A few of these are "delish," which is short for delicious, "yum-o," which is a short exclamation to express how yummy something is, and "sammies," which is short for sandwiches.

Do you recognize any of these words? All of them have found their way into thousands (if not millions) of households across the country and world. As Rachael's popularity increases, these words are only going to be used more and more. It wouldn't be surprising if other television cooks worldwide began using these phrases as common kitchen terminology!

Endless Fame

During the past decade, Rachael has won plenty of awards for her outstanding performance on television. In addition to the Daytime Emmy Award she won in 2006, she won two more in 2008 and 2009 for Outstanding Talk Show/Entertainment. Rachael's face has also showed up in magazine articles, interviews, and television shows. Her straightforward, honest attitude made *Forbes* magazine name her the number-two "most-trusted celebrity" in 2006. (Tom Hanks was number one.)

Rachael also appeared on the popular Food Network show *Iron Chef*. She was teamed with Mario Batali, a famous chef. The secret ingredient was cranberries, so they had to make several dishes including that ingredient. She was very nervous about competing

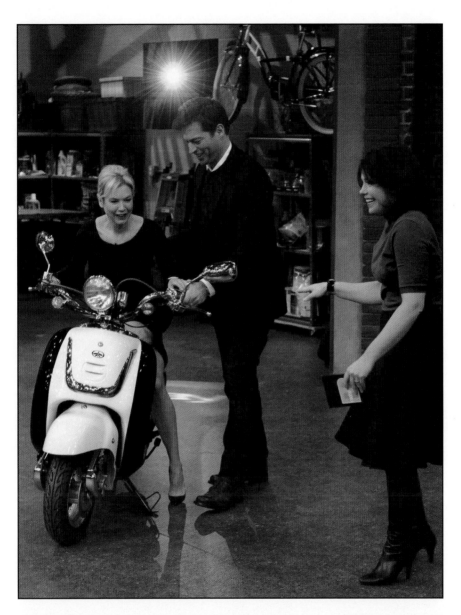

Renée Zellweger and Harry Connick, Jr. on the set of Rachael Ray.

against more professional cooks, but her team managed to win, a true victory for the unconventional cook!

Rachael has also appeared as a guest on many talk shows, including *The View*, *The Today Show*, *The Tonight Show with Jay Leno*, *The Late Show with David Letterman*, *Nightline*, *Late Night with Conan O'Brien*, *Larry King Live*, *Cake Boss*, and *The Late Late Show with Craig Ferguson*. For Sesame Street's thirty-eighth season, Rachael was in an episode to present "pumpernickel" as the word of the day.

On January 12, 2008, Rachael's television series *Rachael's Vacation* premiered on the Food Network; the show is a five-part food travelogue shot in various European countries. Also in 2008, Rachael

Rachael has had amazing celebrity guests on her show. Everyone from Jennifer Lopez to former president Bill Clinton has stopped by to talk with Rachael!

became a producer; she produced the Latin cooking show on the Food Network called *Viva Daisy!*, which starred Daisy Martínez.

In August 2009, Rachael appeared as herself on *Who Wants to Be a Millionaire* with Regis Philbin. The money she earned went to Yum-o! and animal rescue. She was also in the hidden camera show *I Get That a Lot*, pretending to be an employee at a dry cleaners. In September 2010, a new show, her first new cooking show in eight years, *Rachael Ray's Week In a Day*, began airing on the Cooking Channel.

In Rachael's Own Words

"Yum-o!" is the sound you make when you eat something really super delicious. It's kind of a combination of "yummy" and "oh wow!" You can't help but smile when you say it because it's such a fun word to say. A big part of the Yum-o! organization is about making cooking and eating something that makes people happy. Food should be delicious, fun and put a smile on your face.

(From Rachael's website, www.yum-o.org)

Giving Back

When Rachael began her shows on the Food Network, she was making hundreds of thousands of dollars. By the time she had her own talk show, she was making much, much more! In 2006, she decided to do something useful with her increased fame and salary by starting her own **nonprofit** charity organization. She named it after the phrase she coined on her shows to express how delicious something is—Yum-o!

Yum-o! is mostly centered around promoting good nutrition and culinary education, but it branches out into many areas of both. Its aim is to help children and families learn how to cook delicious, nutritious meals on a budget, while also working to feed poor children in our own country. The charity also helps kids in need through awarding scholarships and financial help to fund education.

Rachael's charity has its own website with plenty of useful resources for children wishing to get involved in the kitchen. There, you can find the three areas Rachael outlines as the most important actions of the organization: cook, feed, and fund. Rachael's strategy here is just like the one on her TV show— make it simple, easy, and fun!

Rachael also owns another company, in addition to her Yum-o! charity. She has a great passion for animals, and in 2008, she released a line of pet food called Nutrish. She came up with the recipe while making food for her own pit bull, Isaboo. In 2010, this line was increased to include dog treats, and it may expand even more in the future. All ingredients are decided upon completely by Rachael herself—and all the proceeds go toward helping at-risk animals. These include victims of abuse, mistreatment, and abandonment. Rachael also has a website dedicated not only to this product line but also to helping at-risk animals. It is named, "Rachael's Rescue," and can be found on her main website.

Product Endorsements

Her fans weren't the only ones who were noticing Rachael's growing popularity. Companies were taking notice too, and they wanted

Rachael's pitbull inspired her to create a line of dog food made from healthy ingredients. Rachael is passionate about great food no matter who's eating it!

to snag her bubbly personality as their spokesperson. It started with Nabisco, a company well known for its cookies and snacks. Rachael became their spokeswoman in 2006. This was followed by several other endorsements, including her affiliation with Dunkin' Donuts and AT&T in 2007. Rachael's recipes were made available for on-the-go situations, and plenty of people loved it!

Criticism of Her Methods

Rachael has never been seen as the typical chef in any sense of the word, and this is what makes her so special. However, some chefs are annoyed with her **nontraditional** approach to cooking. A few of them have had plenty of unpleasant things to say about her methods.

First, they don't like her claim that her meals only take thirty minutes to make. A lot of the time, critics point out, her recipes can take much longer, defeating the purpose of her claim that they are quick and easy. She stands behind her claim that if you work quickly, it can be done in thirty minutes. Taking your time will obviously make the meal take longer to prepare.

Second, some critics don't like her lack of precise measuring. As a cook, she doesn't measure in a traditional way. She'll add a "pinch" or a "palmful," but never a teaspoon or cup. She says she doesn't like measuring because doing so takes away from the fun and unexpected element of cooking. "Eyeing it" is a more fun and accurate method for her. That's why Rachael has never liked baking: because baking absolutely does require very precise measurements. Rachael often describes herself as being bad at baking and almost never attempts it.

In 2007, Rachael partnered with Dunkin' Donuts to promote the company's products in commercials.

Other critics don't take her seriously because of her creative terminology. They find the vocabulary she uses to be somewhat childish and unprofessional. Her fans, on the other hand, find it adorable and relatable. Again, her program is meant to be fun and engaging—not a boring documentary! Rachael's personality takes out some of the dryness we are used to seeing in some cooking shows.

Last of all, some critics don't appreciate the way Rachael completely skipped many of the steps her colleagues needed to go through before they could call themselves chefs. They say she doesn't deserve to be so popular.

Rachael married husband John Cusimano in 2005. The two were married in Italy.

It's no wonder some chefs are a little jealous of her success—and maybe their jealousy is behind some of their criticisms. Her former colleague, Mario Batali, who was also her partner on an episode of *Iron Chef*, is a learned chef who embraces Rachael's differences. He praises her calmness and her ability to use her bubbly personality to pull her audience out of buying precooked meals and into cooking their own meals. No matter what her methods are, they're working—and that's what's important! Her victory is a victory for all chefs who are passionate about encouraging people to make their own home-cooked meals.

Personal Life

All this activity has made Rachael a busy girl! Between hosting television shows, writing cookbooks, managing a charity organization, and fulfilling other commitments, it's been hard for her to have the chance to simply enjoy her life. Regardless, she always finds time to retreat back to her roots in upstate New York. She visits whenever she can find a free day or two. Rachael has admitted that she enjoys the quiet, cozy retreat of her upstate home. It's very different from the hustle and bustle of the city life.

In 2005, Rachael married her fiancé, John Cusimano, in a ceremony in Tuscany, Italy. They both describe their relationship with each other as love at first sight. John is both a lawyer and a member of the rock band "The Cringe," based out of New York City. Although not extremely popular, the band's indie rock sound has given it a well-established fan base. The couple owns homes in both upstate New York and New York City, which they travel between as they can.

Tomorrow

The future is looking very bright for Rachael. In only a decade, she has gone from being virtually unknown to being an influential celebrity. She has branched out from her television personality into many different areas, including charity work, product endorsement, and writing her own books and magazines.

Where will she go from here? No one knows for sure! Her recipes and methods may change with the times, and that would continue her success as an innovative, people person.

When you look at Rachael's success, it's hard to remember that she never completed college. Despite this, she still has a very strong opinion about education—so strong, in fact, that part of her organization's charity money goes towards scholarships and educational programs. Ironically, most of her programs involve culinary expertise, something she did not learn in school. But Rachael understands herself. She is aware of what she knows and doesn't know. She just wants to help teach people what she does know.

If Rachael's enthusiasm and passion had lead her in another direction, a direction for which she would have needed a college degree, you can bet she would have completed college. But that's not what happened. Instead, she found herself pulled in another direction.

If you asked Rachael what she thinks about a college education, she'd probably say, "Do whatever makes you happy—and then work as hard as you have to and learn everything you need

About Yum-O!

COOK—*Educating kids and their families about food and cooking*
Yum-o! educates kids and their families about food and cooking, enabling them to get started in the kitchen while making meals that are easy, healthy, affordable and delicious.

FEED—*Feeding hungry American kids*
Despite living in the world's richest country, a startling number of Americans go hungry every year. According to a study completed by the UDSA in 2006, the rate of food insecurity for American households in 2005 was 11%, which means that more than 35 million people did not have access to enough food to meet their basic needs. Nearly 13 million of these people were children—that's almost 1 in 5 kids! These food insecure and hungry kids can be found in urban and rural areas in all geographic regions of the country. They are raised in dual and single parent homes and represent all races and ethnicities.

Hunger in America has been, and continues to be, a real problem for a significant part of our population. Therefore, Yum-o! is making the fight against hunger a part of our mission by partnering with organizations such as Share Our Strength® (SOS) in support of their leading priority: ending childhood hunger in America. Yum-o! also works with organizations throughout the country to raise awareness about and contribute to special projects that address this issue.

FUND – *Funding cooking education and scholarships*
Yum-o! recognizes the wide variety of restaurant and foodservice industry opportunities for young people making career choices today. Yum-o! helps kids reach their food-related career goals by funding scholarships and recognizing public schools that are offering food or nutrition programs that incorporate healthy choices. We accomplish this through our partnerships with the National Restaurant Association Educational Foundation and the Alliance for a Healthier Generation. (From www.yum-o.org)

Rachael has continued to write books, work in television, and run her magazine Everyday. *Rachael seems to be able to do it all!*

to know to be a success." If that takes enrolling at college, then that's great. If not. . .

Well, Rachael is living proof that you can be successful without a college degree!

WHAT CAN YOU EXPECT?

Of course not everyone who skips college is going to be a celebrity or a millionaire. But there are other more ordinary jobs out there for people who choose to go a different route from college. Here's what you can expect to make in 100 of the top-paying jobs available to someone who has only a high school diploma. (If you're not sure what any of the jobs are, look them up on the Internet to find out more about them.) Keep in mind that these are average salaries; a beginning worker will likely make much less, while someone with many more years of experience could make much more. Also, remember that wages for the same jobs vary somewhat in different parts of the country.

Position	Average Annual Salary
rotary drill operators (oil & gas)	$59,560
commercial divers	$58,060
railroad conductors & yardmasters	$54,900
chemical plant & system operators	$54,010
real estate sales agents	$53,100
subway & streetcar operators	$52,800
postal service clerks	$51,670
pile-driver operators	$51,410
railroad brake, signal & switch operators	$49,600

brickmasons & blockmasons	$49,250
postal service mail carriers	$48,940
gaming supervisors	$48,920
postal service mail sorters & processors	$48,260
gas compressor & gas pumping station operators	$47,860
roof bolters (mining)	$47,750
forest fire fighters	$47,270
private detectives & investigators	$47,130
tapers	$46,880
continuous mining machine operators	$46,680
rail car repairers	$46,430
shuttle car operators	$46,400
rail-track laying & maintenance equipment operators	$46,000
chemical equipment operators & tenders	$45,100
explosives workers (ordnance handling experts & blasters)	$45,030
makeup artists (theatrical & performance)	$45,010
sheet metal workers	$44,890
managers/supervisors of landscaping & groundskeeping workers	$44,080
loading machine operators (underground mining)	$43,970
rough carpenters	$43,640

derrick operators (oil & gas)	$43,590
flight attendants	$43,350
refractory materials repairers (except brickmasons)	$43,310
production, planning & expediting clerks	$43,260
mine cutting & channeling machine operators	$43,120
fabric & apparel patternmakers	$42,940
service unit operators (oil, gas, & mining)	$42,690
tile & marble setters	$42,450
paperhangers	$42,310
bridge & lock tenders	$41,630
hoist & winch operators	$41,620
carpet installers	$41,560
pump operators (except wellhead pumpers)	$41,490
terrazzo workers & finishers	$41,360
plasterers & stucco masons	$41,260
painters (transportation equipment)	$41,220
automotive body & related repairers	$41,020
hazardous materials removal workers	$40,270
bailiffs	$40,240
wellhead pumpers	$40,210
maintenance workers (machinery)	$39,570
truck drivers (heavy & tractor-trailer)	$39,260

floor layers (except carpet, wood & hard tiles)	$39,190
managers of retail sales workers	$39,130
cargo & freight agents	$38,940
metal-refining furnace operators & tenders	$38,830
excavating & loading machine and dragline operators	$38,540
separating, filtering, clarifying & still machine operators	$38,450
motorboat operators	$38,390
dredge operators	$38,330
lay-out workers (metal & plastic)	$38,240
forest fire inspectors & prevention specialists	$38,180
medical & clinical laboratory technicians	$37,860
tire builders	$37,830
dental laboratory technicians	$37,690
paving, surfacing & tamping equipment operators	$37,660
locksmiths & safe repairers	$37,550
sailors & marine oilers	$37,310
dispatchers (except police, fire & ambulance)	$37,310
pipelayers	$37,040
helpers (extraction workers)	$36,870

rolling machine setters, operators & tenders	$36,670
welders, cutters & welder fitters	$36,630
solderers & brazers	$36,630
gem & diamond workers	$36,620
police, fire & ambulance dispatchers	$36,470
models	$36,420
meter readers (utilities)	$36,400
mechanical door repairers	$36,270
public address system & other announcers	$36,130
rail yard engineers, dinkey operators & hostlers	$36,090
bus drivers (transit & intercity)	$35,990
insurance policy processing clerks	$35,740
insurance claims clerks	$35,740
computer-controlled machine tool operators (metal and plastic)	$35,570
license clerks	$35,570
court clerks	$35,570
fallers	$35,570
septic tank servicers & sewer pipe cleaners	$35,470
parking enforcement workers	$35,360
highway maintenance workers	$35,310
floor sanders & finishers	$35,140

tool grinders, filers, & sharpeners	$35,110
paper goods machine setters, operators & tenders	$35,040
printing machine operators	$35,030
inspectors, testers, sorters, samplers & weighers	$34,840
pourers & casters (metal)	$34,760
loan interviewers & clerks	$34,670
furnace, kiln, oven, drier & kettle operators & tenders	$34,410
recreational vehicle service technicians	$34,320
roustabouts (oil & gas)	$34,190

Source: Bureau of Labor Statistics, U.S. Department of Labor, 2008.

Find Out More

In Books

Abrams, Dennis. *Rachael Ray: Food Entrepreneur.* New York: Chelsea House, 2009.

Keedle, Jayne. *Rachael Ray: People We Should Know.* New York: Gareth Stevens, 2009.

Ray, Rachael. *Cooking Rocks! Rachael Ray 30-Minute Meals for Kids.* New York: Lake Isle Press, 2004.

———. *Yum-O! The Family Cookbook.* New York: Clarkson Potter, 2008.

On the Internet

Every Day with Rachael Ray
www.rachaelraymag.com

Rachael Ray Kids
www.rachaelray.com/kids

Yum-O!
www.yum-o.org

Disclaimer

The websites listed on this page were active at the time of publication. The publisher is not responsible for websites that have changed their address or discontinued operation since the date of publication. The publisher will review and update the websites upon each reprint.

Index

Picture Credits

Abdul Sami Haqqani | Dreamstime.com: 16
Adogslifephoto | Dreamstime.com: p. 47
Cape Cod Tourism: p. 12
Clarkson Potter: p. 38
Daniel Case: p. 15
Daniel Schwen: p.18
Everyday with Rachael Ray: pp. 36, 28, 40, 54
JBC3: p. 11
Lake Isle Press: pp. 32, 34,
Mark Williamson | Dreamstime.com: p. 49
Noah Strycker | Dreamstime.com: p. 22
Six Train: p. 21
Stephen Coburn | Dreamstime.com: p.25
The Heart Truth: p. 8

To the best knowledge of the publisher, all images not specifically credited are in the public domain. If any image has been inadvertently uncredited, please notify Harding House Publishing Services, 220 Front Street, Vestal, New York 13850, so that credit can be given in future printings.

About the Author

Shaina Carmel Indovino is a writer and illustrator living in Nesconset, New York. She graduated from Binghamton University, where she received degrees in sociology and English.